Published by Stirred Stories
First Edition: November 2021

The Butcher, the Baker, and the Candlestick Maker

A Shabbat Story

by **Jennifer Winters**

Illustrated by
Michelle Nahmad

It was Friday afternoon, and little Nathan raced home from school through the city streets to see how his mama was feeling. She had a terrible cold that started two days before.

As he got closer to his building, he didn't see his mama looking out their third-floor window as usual. (She liked to watch out the window to make sure he crossed the street safely.)

Nathan ran up the steps, into the apartment, and down the hall to his parents' bedroom. Mama was in her bed, surrounded by half-full cups of tea, an oozing honey jar, and piles of tissues that looked like snowballs.

"How are you feeling, Mama?" Nathan whispered softly, peeking into her room. In a hoarse and scratchy voice, she said, "I'm still not feeling so hotsy-totsy."

Nathan liked it when she said "hotsy-totsy." It made not feeling so good sound a whole lot better.

"You are so sweet to ask," said Mama. "But we now have a little problem. Daddy is still at work. It is getting close to Shabbat. I haven't been able to do my shopping yet."

Mama sounded worried. Nathan dropped his backpack, eager to help. "What do we need, Mama? I can do the shopping."

"We need a plump and juicy chicken from the Butcher,

a fresh and warm challah from the Baker,

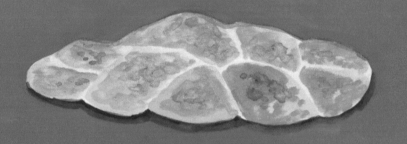

and two white candles from the Candlestick Maker," Mama told him.

Nathan smiled. He knew he could do it.

Mama gave Nathan detailed directions to find the shops. Nathan told her not to worry—he'd gone shopping with her before and knew the way. "I won't let you down," Nathan assured her.

Mama gave Nathan a bulging tan leather wallet that clasped at the top. Filled with money, it fit tightly in his pocket.

Nathan went to the cabinet to get three grocery bags, then ran back to say goodbye. With the money in his pocket and the bags in his hand, Nathan kissed his mama's warm keppe. Then he turned and skipped out the door, yelling "Don't worry, Mama, I'll be back in plenty of time to prepare for Shabbat!"

"Be careful!" she called after him. Nathan didn't answer—he was confident he could do this all on his own.

Out he went into the bustling city streets filled with people rushing here and there. Everything felt much bigger when he was out in the city alone, but he was determined to help his mama.

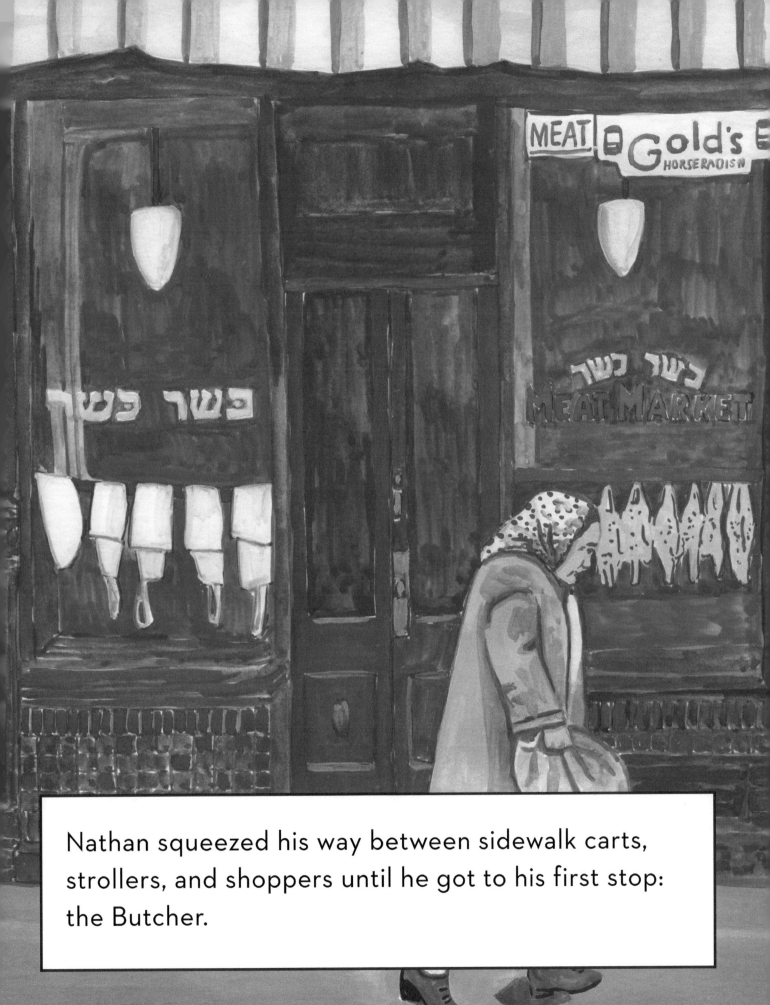

Nathan squeezed his way between sidewalk carts, strollers, and shoppers until he got to his first stop: the Butcher.

It was crowded at the butcher shop. The people were as tall and loud as trees in a forest on a stormy night. Nathan felt scared and small. But he had to be brave:

Mama was counting on his help to prepare for Shabbat. Nathan reached up to take a ticket. It read: Number 56. He shyly stepped back and waited for his number to be called.

When the Butcher finally called out "Number 56!" Nathan walked up to the large glass counter, stood on his tippy-toes, and tried to peer over the top. He could barely see the Butcher—and the Butcher couldn't see him!

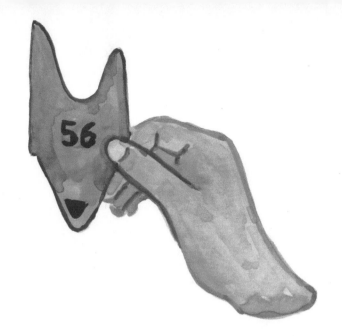

The Butcher called again: "Number 56! Where's number 56?" and Nathan hopped up and down to catch his eye.

When the Butcher saw him, he leaned over the counter to meet him halfway. "Well hello there, Nathan! What can I get you?" he said. Nathan was relieved that the Butcher recognized him. He replied in a timid voice, "Please, my mama is sick. I need a plump and juicy chicken for Shabbat dinner."

The Butcher handed him a heavy round package wrapped in shiny white paper. He said, "Give this plump and juicy chicken to your mama and tell her I hope she gets well soon."

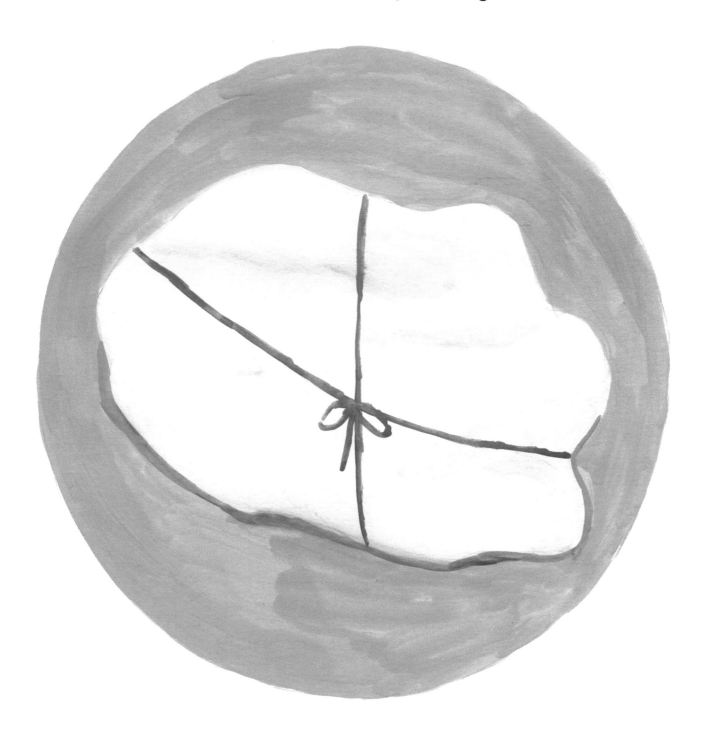

The chicken was so large, Nathan needed some help getting it into his bag. He promised to deliver the message with the chicken to his mama.

Nathan reached into his pocket, yanked out the wallet, and unclasped it.

After paying, he pinched the wallet closed, stuffed it back into his pocket, and thanked the Butcher. As he turned to leave, he smiled—he knew he wasn't going to let his mama down.

Nathan left the butcher shop and set off towards the Baker with a spring in his step. The bakery was only two blocks away, and he could practically smell the freshly baked challah from where he stood.

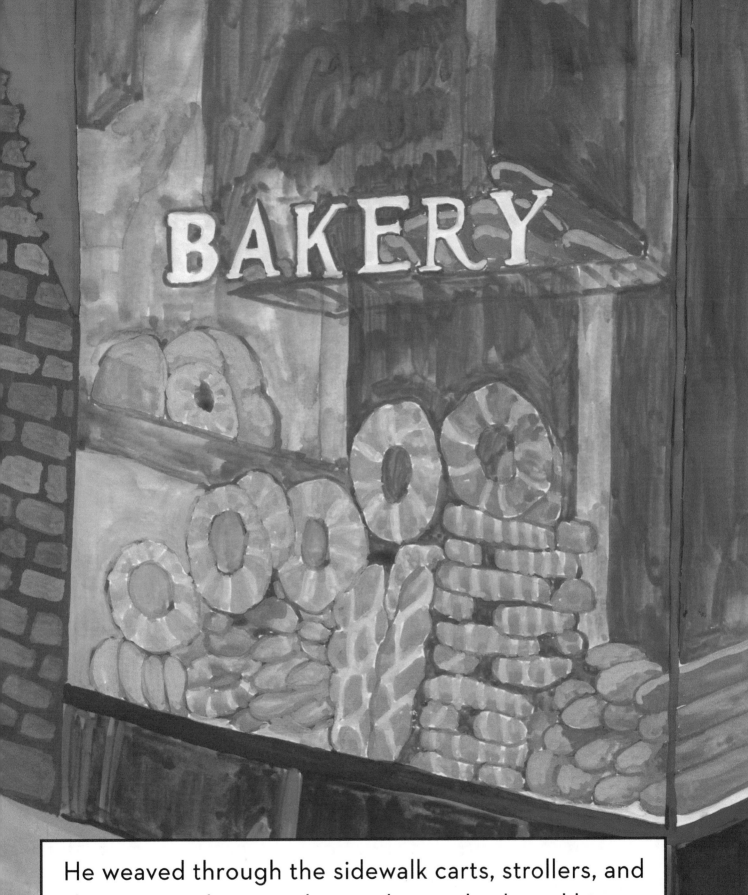

He weaved through the sidewalk carts, strollers, and shoppers with ease—they no longer bothered him, for he knew exactly where to go.

When Nathan opened the door to the bakery, he saw that it was just as crowded as the butcher shop! He took a deep breath to calm his nerves.

Nathan got in line and waited. People were buying up all the challah: the loaves seemed to be disappearing right in front of his eyes! Nathan nervously wondered if there would be any left by the time he got to the front of the line.

When it was his turn, he stepped toward the counter, but the Baker looked right over his head! Nathan stood on his tippy-toes and waved to get the Baker's attention.

When he saw him, the Baker leaned over his counter and said, "Well hello there, Nathan! What can I get you?"

Relieved that the Baker recognized him, he replied, "Please, my mama is sick. I need a fresh and warm challah for the Shabbat blessing."

The Baker handed Nathan a golden challah that smelled so delicious it made him want to carve a tunnel through it and hide inside its sweet-smelling warmth.

"This is the last challah, fresh from the oven," the Baker told him. "Give it to your mama and tell her I hope she gets well soon."

Nathan was so relieved to get the very last freshly baked challah for Shabbat! Carefully, gently, he placed it in his second grocery bag.

"I promise to deliver your message with the challah to my mama," Nathan said as he reached into his pocket and yanked out the wallet. He undid the clasp and paid the Baker. Then he stuffed the wallet back into his pocket and said, "Thank you, Shabbat Shalom!"

Nathan was so proud of himself. He knew he was being a great help to his mama. But when Nathan left the bakery, he noticed something: the streets were no longer crowded. The sidewalk carts were packing up, the strollers were gone, and the last of the shoppers were heading home.

He looked up and saw the sun was setting in the sky. "Oh no!" he thought. "It must be getting close to Shabbat. I'd better get home!"

He walked as fast as he could with his heavy bundles weighing him down, retracing his steps back towards home. Suddenly, he stopped—checking his shopping bags, he realized he still had one left over. He must have forgotten something, but poor Nathan couldn't remember what it was!

Nathan was crushed. For the first time, he started to worry that he might let his mama down. He stopped on the side of the street and went through his bags.

He checked the first bag and saw the chicken—he'd already been to the Butcher. He looked in the second bag and saw the challah—he'd already been to the Baker. But where was he supposed to go next?

Now Nathan was getting discouraged. He looked up and down the block for a familiar face, but no one was around to ask for help. Unsure what to do, he looked up.

The setting sun was bright and fiery, glowing many shades of orange in the darkening sky.

"Ah ha! The Candlestick Maker!" Nathan exclaimed.

Nathan ran through the emptying streets and reached the Candlestick Maker's shop in no time. He walked right in, went straight up to the counter, stood on his tippy-toes, and said, "HELLO!"

"Well hello Nathan," said the Candlestick Maker. "Good timing, I was just about to close. What can I get you?"

"My mama is sick," Nathan replied. "I need two white candlesticks to welcome Shabbat, please."

The Candlestick Maker gracefully picked out two beautiful white candlesticks. "Take these to your mama," he said.

"Tell her I hope they bring your family warmth, health, and happiness this Shabbat."

Nathan promised he would deliver the message with the candlesticks to his mama. He reached into his pocket and yanked out the wallet.

Much to Nathan's surprise, it was already open—and it was empty.

"Oh, no!" thought Nathan. The money had fallen out of the wallet. He must have forgotten to pinch the clasp after paying the Baker!

Looking up at the Candlestick Maker with watery eyes, Nathan showed him the empty wallet. "All my money is gone. I have nothing left and cannot buy the candlesticks for our Shabbat table."

Once again, Nathan felt like he was alone in a dark forest on a stormy night. The wind shook the trees and blew his confidence away. With his shoulders slumped, holding back tears, Nathan turned to leave. But before he reached the door, the Candlestick Maker called him back.

"Nathan, wait. You are helping your mama and I want to help you." He held out the candlesticks. "Take these home for Shabbat. It's my gift to you and your family." Nathan wiped his eyes, overwhelmed by this act of kindness, and thanked the Candlestick Maker. "Enjoy the warmth and light," said the Candlestick Maker, "and have a peaceful Shabbat."
Nathan carefully placed the candlesticks into his third bag, thanked the Candlestick Maker again, and set off towards home.

As he turned onto his street, Nathan was delighted by what he saw—his mama was sitting in her chair at the window, waiting for him! She must be feeling a little better.

Nathan walked up the steps to his apartment carefully, so as not to break the candlesticks. When he got inside, he saw that Papa was already home. Papa had put a pot of water on the stove, where it sat boiling, ready for the chicken. Papa took the heavy bundles from Nathan's tired little hands, tousled his hair, and whispered, "well done."

Mama gave Nathan a warm hug and kissed him on his keppe. Nathan took a deep breath and filled his lungs with her familiar sweet, honey scent.

"Mama, I have messages from the Butcher, the Baker, and the Candlestick Maker. They all hope you get well soon and that our family has a Shabbat filled with warmth, health, and happiness."

Nathan was pleased—he had delivered the packages and greetings as promised.

But he had one more thing to say.

"There is something else I have to tell you, Mama. I lost the money you gave me for the candlesticks. It must have fallen out when I left the Baker. The Candlestick Maker gave them to me because he knew I was trying to help you, so he helped me." Nathan sniffled. "I'm sorry I lost the money. I didn't want to let you down."

Mama put her hand on his shoulder. "Don't worry about that now. We all have to take care of each other. You have never let me down."

Nathan smiled and wiped away his tears. His mama gave him a hug. "I am so proud of you for helping our family today."

Mama and Nathan cleaned up the tissues and the honey, put away the teacups, and set the table. Papa gently lowered the chicken into the boiling pot for soup. At the table, Nathan and Mama set the challah on a cutting board and covered it with an embroidered cloth.

Feeling grateful for each other, the family lit the Shabbat candles together.

Jennifer Winters

Jennifer Winters is a former reading and elementary educator who loved helping her students discover their family backgrounds while enhancing their reading skills. She is also a perpetual student as she continues to learn and develop her own family tree. Living near New York City gives her the benefit of retracing the cultural footsteps of her immigrant grandparents, great grandparents, and extended family. The Butcher, the Baker, and the Candlestick Maker, Jennifer's second children's book, is a compilation of memories from her own family's rich history.

Michelle Nahmad

Coming from generations of immigrants from Syria, Panama, Poland, Russia, and Costa Rica, Michelle Nahmad examines culture and explores history in her illustration, design, and narrative work. Originally from Miami, Florida, Michelle now lives in Brooklyn, New York. You can also find her at michellenahmad.com.

CPSIA information can be obtained
at www.ICGtesting.com
Printed in the USA
LVHW070934240222
711906LV00003B/70